CHRIS GRINE
CHICKENHARE

graphix

AN IMPRINT OF

SCHOLASTIC

ALL RIGHTS RESERVED. PUBLISHED BY GRAPHIX, A DIVISION OF SCHOLASTIC
INC., *PUBLISHERS SINCE 1920*. SCHOLASTIC AND ASSOCIATED LOGOS ARE
TRADEMARKS AND/OR REGISTERED TRADEMARKS OF SCHOLASTIC INC.

NO PART OF THIS PUBLICATION MAY BE REPRODUCED, STORED IN A
RETRIEVAL SYSTEM, OR TRANSMITTED IN ANY FORM OR BY ANY MEANS,
ELECTRONIC, MECHANICAL, PHOTOCOPYING, RECORDING, OR OTHERWISE,
WITHOUT WRITTEN PERMISSION OF THE PUBLISHER. FOR INFORMATION
REGARDING PERMISSION, WRITE TO SCHOLASTIC INC., ATTENTION:
PERMISSIONS DEPARTMENT, 557 BROADWAY, NEW YORK, NY 10012.

LIBRARY OF CONGRESS CONTROL NUMBER: 2012936214

ISBN 978-0-545-48508-1
12 11 10 9 8 7 6 5 4 3 2 1   13 14 15 16 17
PRINTED IN CHINA   38

FIRST EDITION, FEBRUARY 2013
BOOK DESIGN BY PHIL FALCO
EDITED BY ADAM RAU
CREATIVE DIRECTOR: DAVID SAYLOR

1

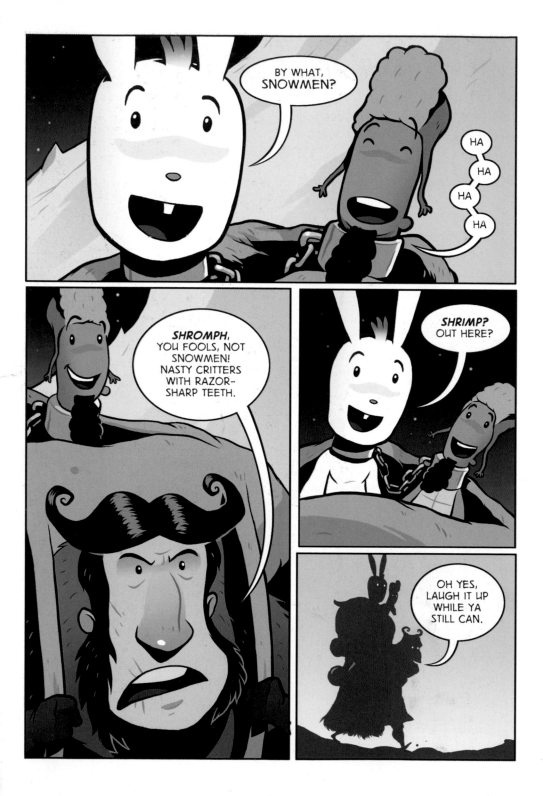

4

5

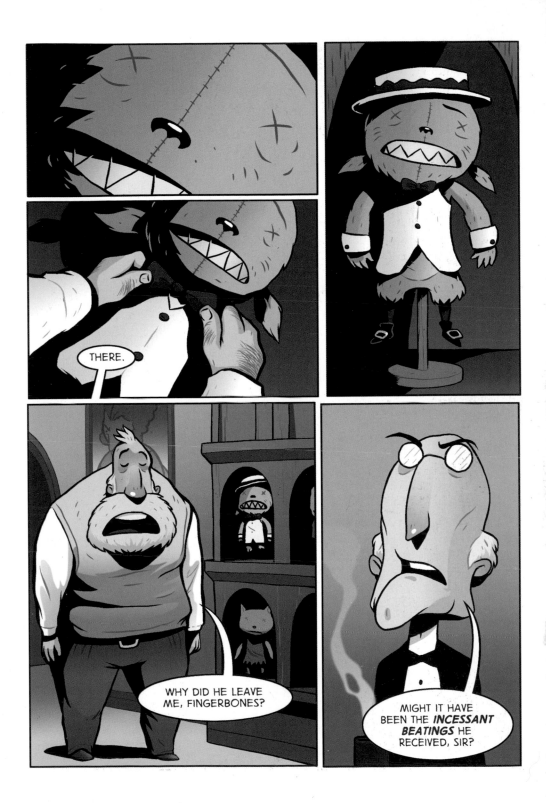

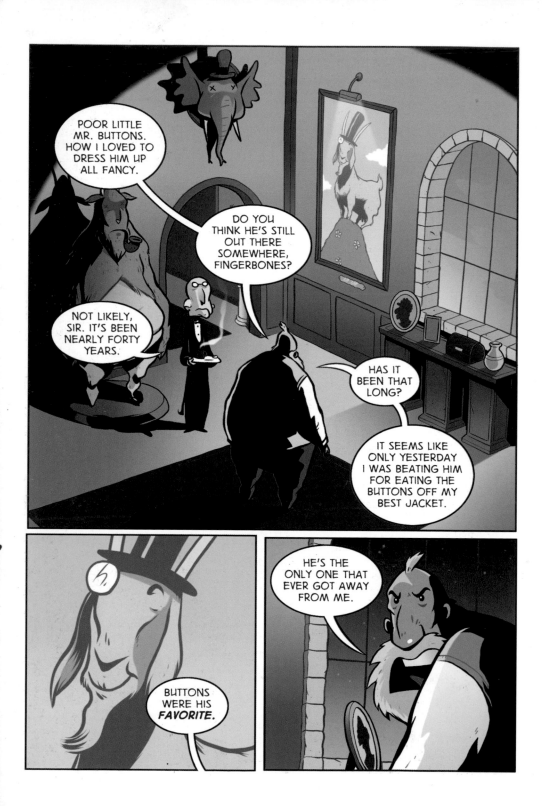

8

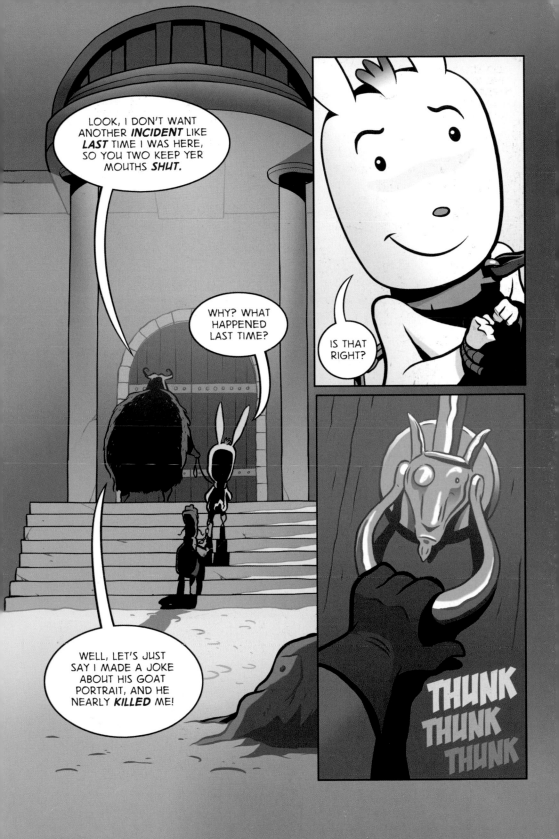

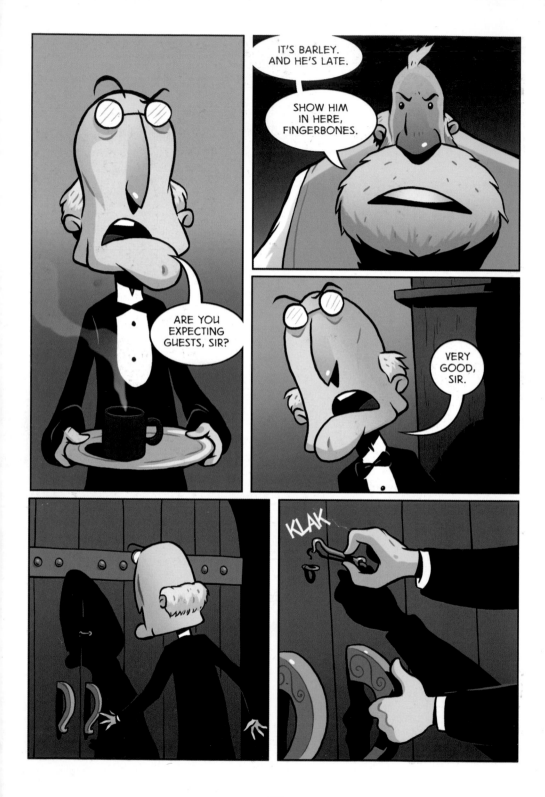

12

15

17

18

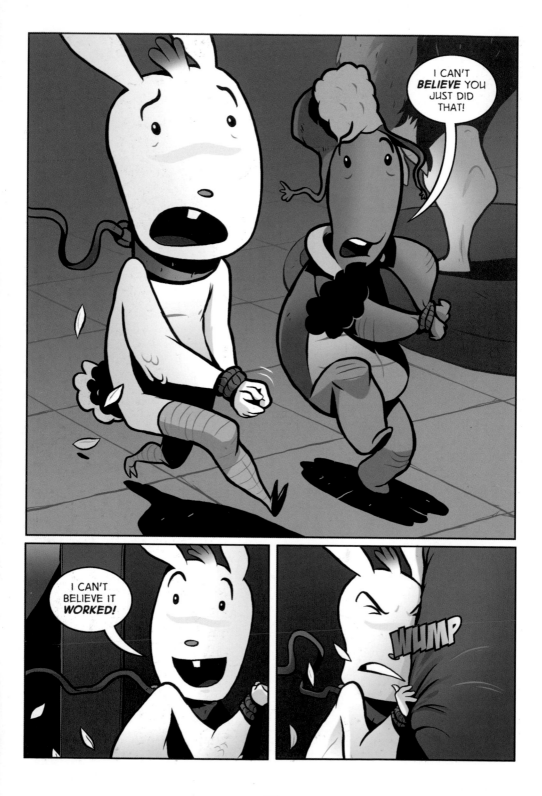

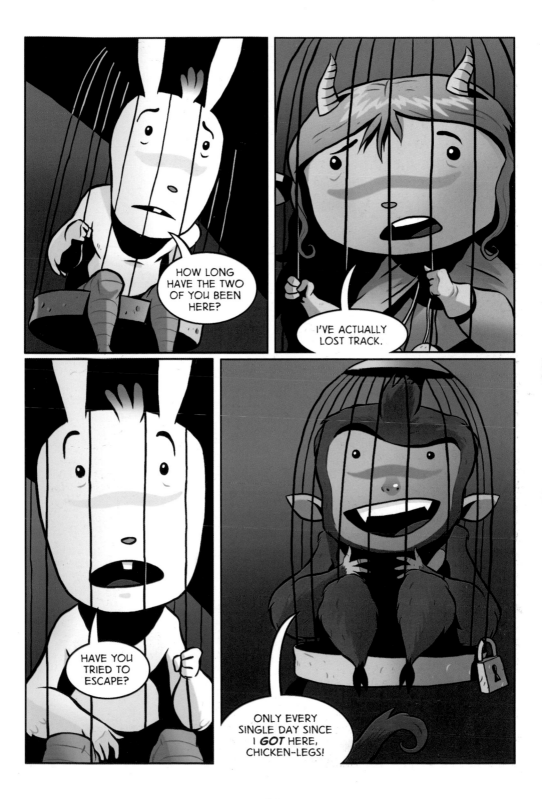

28

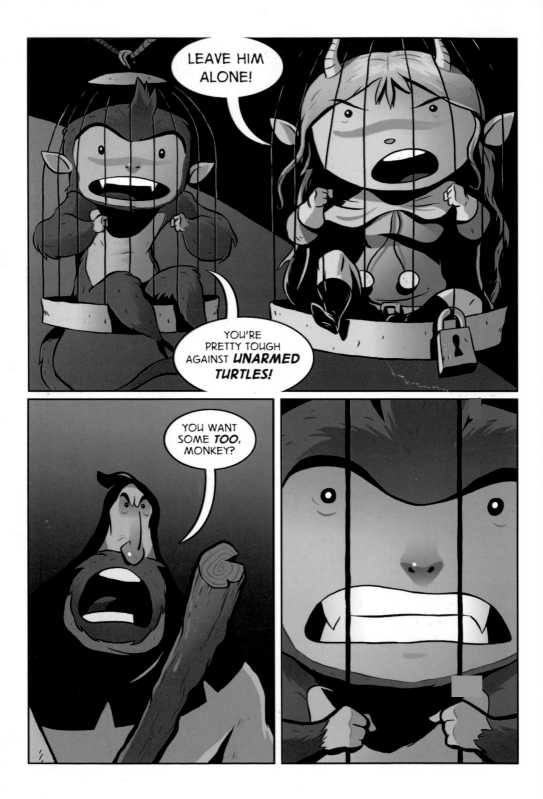

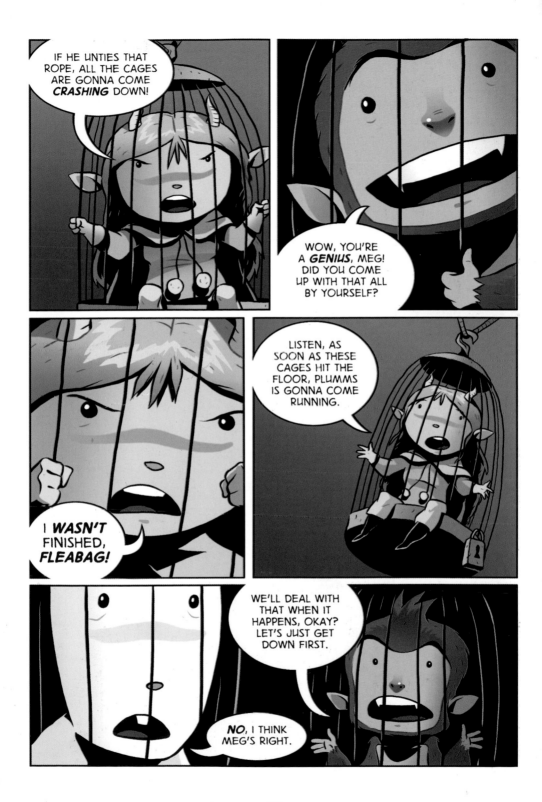

WELL, *LOOKY* WHAT I FOUND OUT HERE ON THIS *TINY* LEDGE.

SO MUCH FOR THAT BIG *ESCAPE* PLAN, HUH?

WHY DON'T YOU JUST COME BACK INSIDE. THERE'S NOWHERE ELSE TO GO EXCEPT DOWN, AND I *DOUBT* YOU WANNA GO *THAT* WAY.

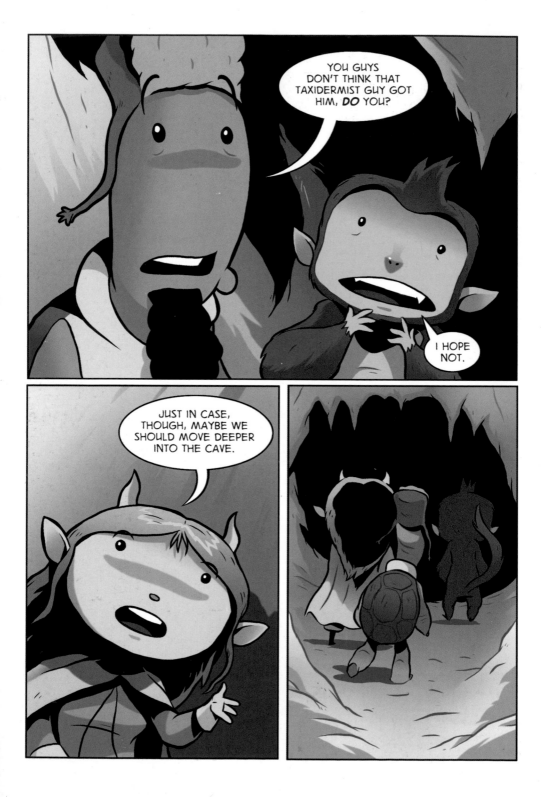

73

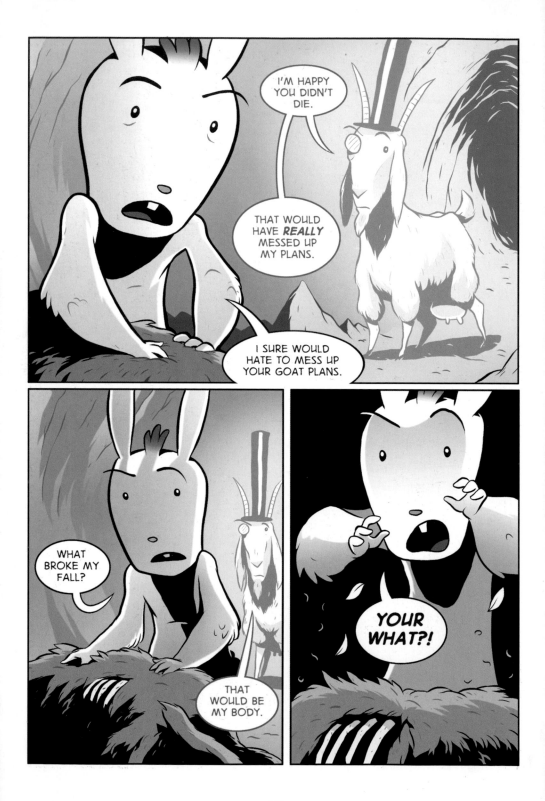

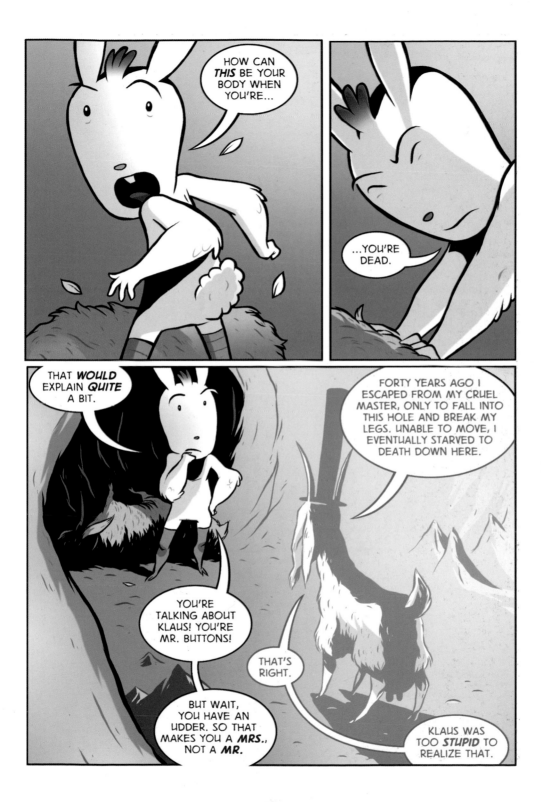

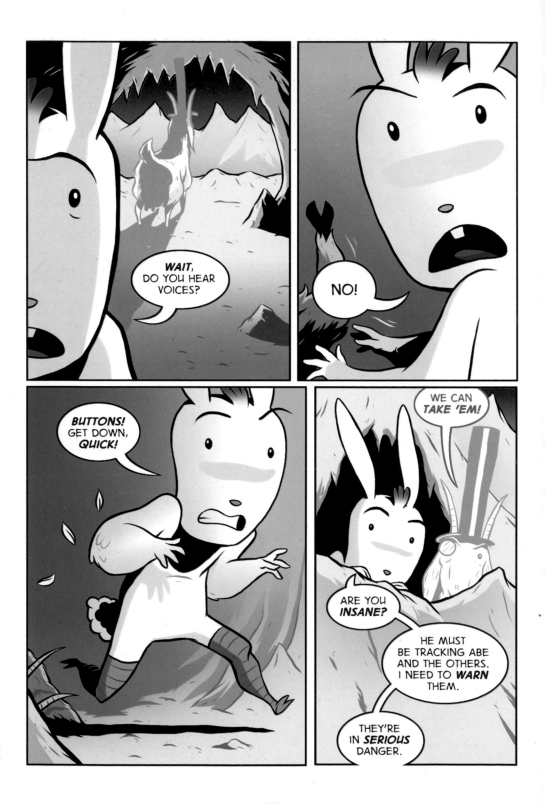

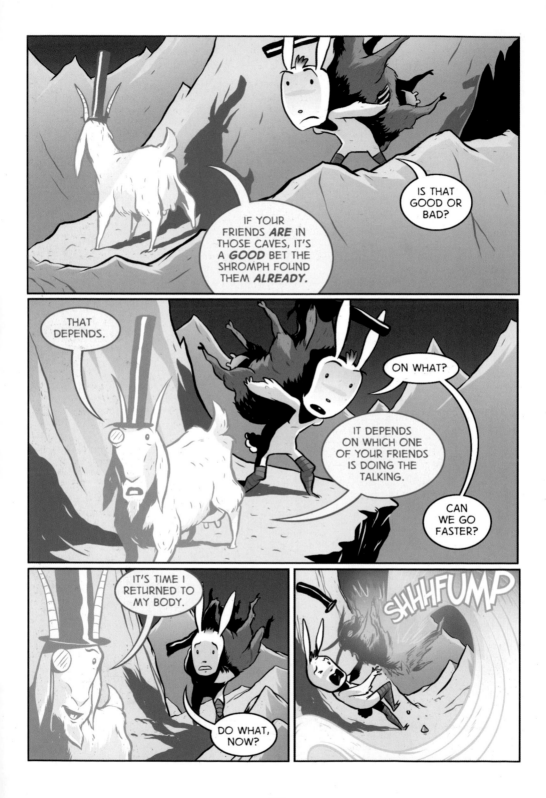

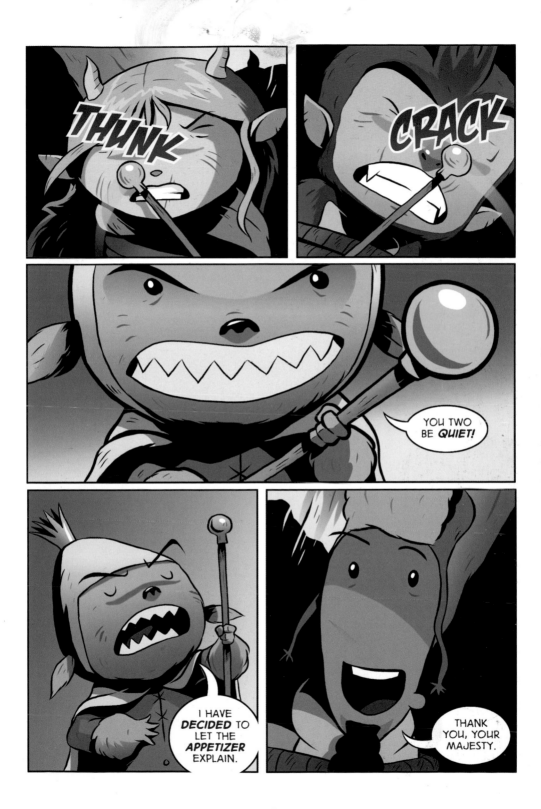

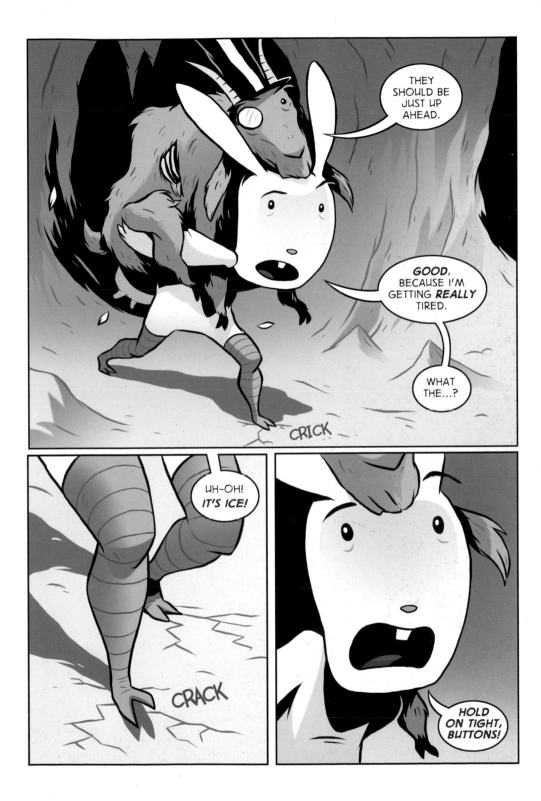

115

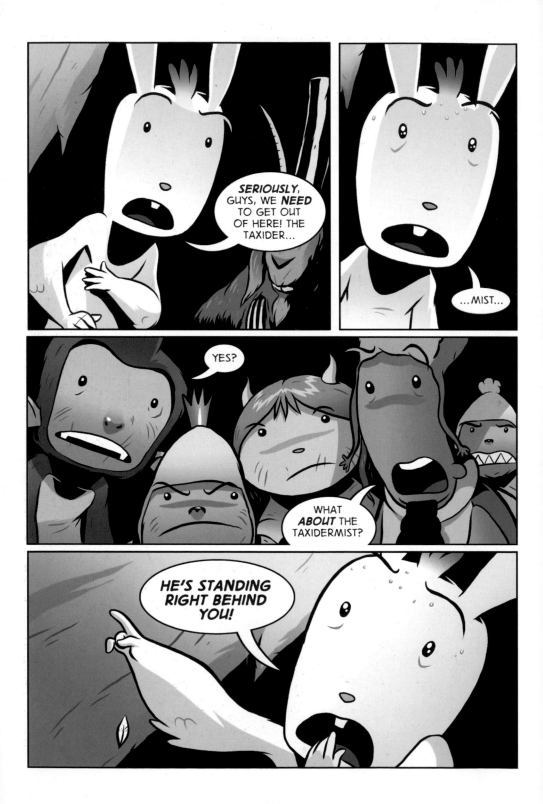

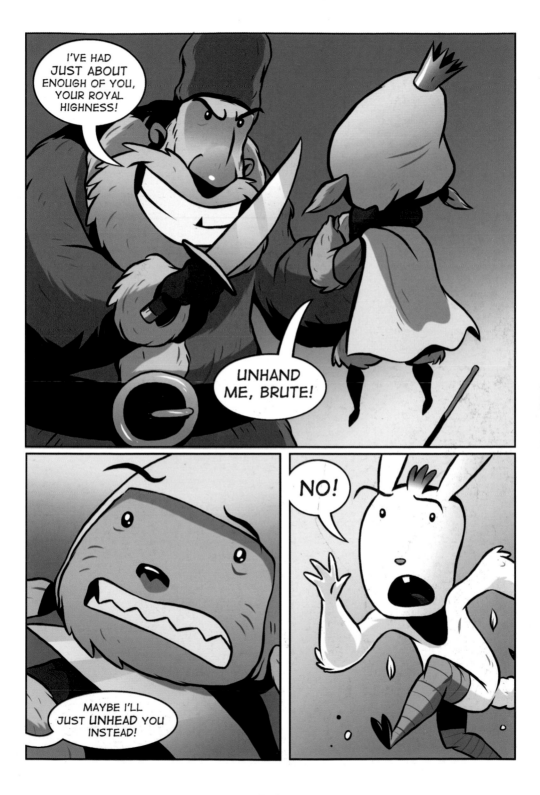

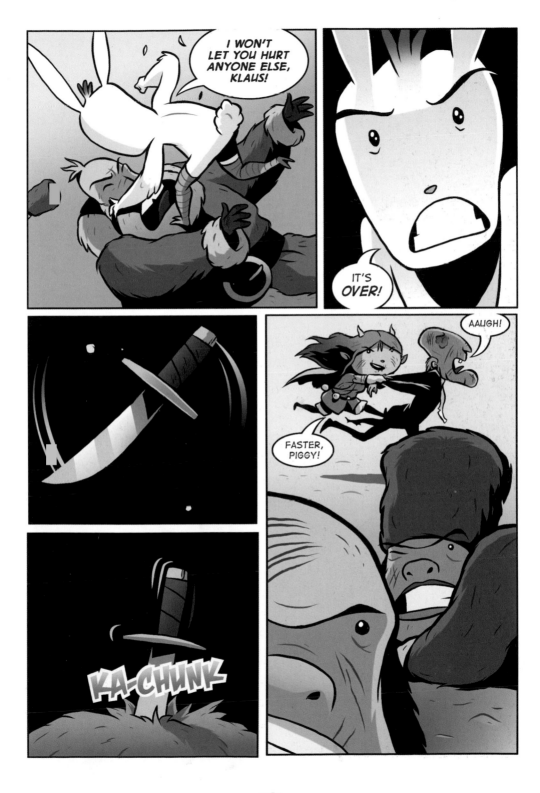

146

148

CHRIS GRINE spent most of his childhood years reading comics and watching cartoons and movies. He attended the Kansas City Art Institute before completing his bachelor's degree in Illustration at Ringling School of Art + Design in 2000. After graduating, he went on to become a greeting card artist at Hallmark Cards in Kansas City, Missouri. It was years later that he realized he could in fact have his career, a family, and time left over in the day to try his luck at comics. *Chickenhare* is the fruit of those efforts.